Cipactli

&

The Glowing Pigs
of El Cenizo

By

Mario E. Martinez

Interior design by Booknook.biz

Cipactli

&

The Glowing Pigs
of El Cenizo

Other Works by Mario E. Martinez

San Casimiro, Texas: Short Stories
Ashtree
A Pig Named Orrenius & Other Strange Tales
NEO-Laredo

This book is dedicated to

Robert E. Howard
&
Hideyuki Kikuchi

I.

He'd seen the sky burn. The bombs pierced the clouds before hitting the rio and vaporizing the waters and a huge chunk of NEO-Laredo along with it. Those who didn't die from the blast or the radiation fled wherever King Gringo's fires couldn't reach. He had nowhere to go. His family had been there for centuries. Young as he was, he still had his pride. If he was to die, it would be on the land of his people.

When the world settled, people returned to NEO-Laredo and he watched the scavengers and squatters grow tumorous and gaunt and die off. The radiation and solitude hadn't hurt him at all. Instead, it made him grow strong, grow fearless, though the transformation was not without its price.

After many years, he saw his face in a mirror while raiding an abandoned house in the El Norte district. Most of his teeth were gone and the natural upturn of his nose was exaggerated, twisted. The reflection shocked him at first, but a man now, he thought if he was alone, it didn't matter what he looked like. His body wasn't like the scavengers he saw either. His was a body of muscle and tumors. His arms were long and lean, hands thick. His skin was coarse and leathery and sat on his bones like wet clay.

Eventually, the pigs came.

It was a few at first. Big heavy things sniffing at the carcass scraps. With nothing more than sharpened sticks and metal pipes, he killed one or two to eat in those early days.

With time though, the wind carried the scent of rot out to the ruined montes of the Frontera. Every day, more and more pigs arrived, walking the streets, enjoying the abandoned markets, ransacking homes for their partially emptied pantries. Originally, the pigs feared him—something about his stench or his shape, perhaps, frightened them, but he kept his distance from the pigs, only following them to steal their food once they'd sniffed it out.

Like him, the pigs weren't bothered by the radiation, even if they gave off bioluminescent glows at night because of it. They seemed to enjoy the contaminated warmth of the dead city. There, the pigs found refuge to grow larger, more vicious, more deformed. Within a generation, coarse bristles covered patches of skin and tusks grew like fangs, sideways or piercing cheeks. Their skins and hair were tinged with a sickly green sheen.

He studied them and noted they had two types. The smaller ones were clever and smart enough to know he could kill them. Those tested him in groups. They hunted him at different times of day—their glow made them easy to spot at night—and attacked from multiple angles. The larger ones could be dealt with until they were in groups, though even the man wouldn't try his luck with one even if it was close. A single mistake against the big ones meant death.

He'd been careful. No pigs were around while he scavenged the old Mines district. He broke into a storage house that had some canned insta-meals and cured meats teetering on rancid. He carried the cans up the main road to the decrepit mansion in El Norte he took for his home. But once he'd cleared the gates of the abandoned neighborhood, he smelled them and heard their squeals among the ruined houses.

The pigs surrounded him but did not attack.

He tossed his bag at them, thinking all they wanted was his food, but they stepped over the insta-meals with indifference.

None of the pigs moved until the largest boar he'd ever seen emerged from one of the side streets. Easily the size of a bull, its legs and shoulders rippled with muscles, and its tusks were almost elephantine. The boar lumbered toward him, jaws clacking in anticipation.

Seeing no escape, the man took his weapon—a piece of rebar with a chunk of concrete attached to one end—from his belt and held it like a warhammer. He gave the surrounding pigs a hard look before roaring at the big boar.

The boar tried to bite him, tried to impale him, but found the man dexterous and agile and his speed was matched by the power of his swings. Though the boar was able to gore the man's thigh and snag bits of cloth in its teeth, with each passing second, its face became more misshapen, its flesh battered and bruised. Soon, it grew tired of biting and spinning and chasing the man who moved like a wild cat.

When the boar was too slow on a turn, the man sprang forward and swung his concrete hammer with both hands. Both boar skull and concrete cracked. The boar dropped, kicking in its death throes, and he was left with only a piece of bent iron. The man leapt onto the fallen beast and stabbed it with abandon until the dead boar's guts were soup on the ground.

He stood over the dead thing. The pigs watched him. Breathless, he glared at them. The man used the sharp end of the rebar to cut the boar's face and break its jaw down the center. He tore the skull from the neck and pulled, straining with all his might, until the skull came away with a large swatch of hide.

He wrapped the bloody skin around him and, one by one, the pigs followed him home.

II.

Pulga napped under the sparce shade of a retama. He'd spent the afternoon on the banks of the rio with his trusted fishing pole. He'd already managed to get a few catfish. One of them was even free of the puckered sores that bloomed on most of the river fish. His mother had told him that, long ago, before King Gringo ruined the world, none of the fish were sick.

By the time he woke, the sun was almost down. Cursing, Pulga hurried to a little pool he'd dug where he'd strung four catfish. He threw them over his shoulder, happy at the cool water soaking into his homespun shirt. Even if his mother wouldn't like the fish smell, she'd forgive him when she saw his haul. They could eat two and sell the others.

His home, El Cenizo, wasn't far off, but with the hills surrounding the riverbank, it was a while before Pulga saw the town walls. They'd been put there, his mother told him, after NEO-Laredo stopped burning and the earth cooled. In the aftermath, the world now ruined, the town had worried about marauders. The walls were irregular—thick in some spots, thin in others—and made of scrap metal and wood from abandoned homes and nearby ranchos. Nopales, their ever-growing ally, were planted at the base of the walls for added defense.

Pulga always thought nopal cactus was beautiful. The way they were always green while the rest of the world withered like straw. Even at dusk, Pulga sleepily thought he saw the green of the nopales as he crested a hill.

But something wasn't right.

It was too dark to see distant nopal patches. And... they glowed and moved like ripples of green water lapping against the walls of El Cenizo. He saw red lasbolts and rifle flares on the walls and was confused.

The sounds found him all at once. The screams, the gun blasts, and the squeals and guttural roars. From the walls, someone threw a torch to light the field and then Pulga saw the truth.

Gigantic pigs glowed a faint green among the nopales. There were hundreds. They thrashed through the cactus patches, knocking down as many arms and paddles as they could before retreating in pain to be replaced by another pig.

Before he could think of what to do, there was rustling to his left. It came from the direction of NEO-Laredo, which made him turn all the faster—since King Gringo scorched the world, NEO-Laredo was thought to be a haunted place where spirits were fused to the land by the heat of the bombs.

No ghosts waited for him though.

It was a boar. A huge one. Pulga only made out the vaguest of outlines, the green sheen to its skin revealing little, but he saw enough to tell it barreled toward him. Pulga was frozen at first but had sense enough to realize the boar had smelled the catfish and threw them as far as he could into the monte.

Pulga ran back toward the rio, to a place he and few of the children called Geronimo's Ditch, named after the drunk found dead in it years ago. It was a pit that, at one end, had a small tunnel where the children often hid things. Though he knew it would be a tight squeeze, there was no other place to hide.

The wet sound of the boar devouring the fish—jaws crunching through bones and lips slathered with blood—made Pulga run faster. He shimmied as deep into the hole as he could. It was dark and cool inside, but just as his pulse slowed, the earth above him grew heavy. The boar tore at the ground above his head and Pulga couldn't control his tears. Still, he didn't dare move.

The snorts of the boar and the shifting of hard clay moving above. The game went on for hours, the chaos and quiet, lulling Pulga into a sense of relief only for the boar to start digging again. The boy wondered if someone would see, only to remember the hole couldn't be seen from the walls of El Cenizo. For Geronimo, it had been buzzards that alerted the town. It was then that Pulga really thought he was going to die.

The second night, Pulga was near delirious. Even underground, the heat of the Frontera couldn't be stopped. The boy's sweat stung his eyes and his mouth was dry. His legs and hips were asleep from being wedged underground for so long. But he had to be still if he wanted to live to see his mother again.

The boar was relentless. It had caught his scent and was ravenous. No snake or root would sate its hunger. It wanted young meat and bones.

Close to the next morning, when the owls stopped their songs and the songbirds started theirs, a tarantula escaping the heat found its way into the hole. Pulga slapped it away and hissed at it.

The boar was there instantly. Though too big to push its way into the hole, its face filled the entrance. Its bites vibrated through Pulga's hiding place. The boar's hot breath stank of rotted meat and catfish. Pulga covered his face against the ropes of slobber and screamed with all that his tired heart could muster.

When he stopped to take in a deep breath, Pulga realized he was the only one making noise. He opened his eyes to the dark and saw the boar's head. It rested on its cheek, eyes open and tongue lolled onto the dirt.

Something pulled the head away from the hole and the hiding place was flooded with light.

"Niño," a gruff voice called. "Are you still alive?"

Pulga watched a brown-skinned arm snake through the entrance of the hiding place. The boy reached for it, felt the rough hand close around his own, and then all was dark.

III.

El Cenizo buried two and prayed to the christ that the missing boy, Pulga La Mantia, would be found unharmed. The funerals were quick affairs since the pigs left little to be buried. All that was left of Señor Guzman was his foot and Señora Barrera's lone arm had been buried in a clean sheet. Guzman had been outside the walls collecting prickly pears by lantern light when the pigs came. The one pig that forced its way through the gates had tackled Señora Barrera and took large bites out of her until it was finally gunned down.

Once the pigs had gone, Dolores La Mantia realized Pulga was missing. The boy usually bounced all over town like a flea— hence his name—but when the chaos ceased, no one could find him. Dolores wanted to rush out of the gates, screaming his name, but the mayor stopped her.

"The pigs could still be out there," he'd pleaded. Some of the men on the wall reported seeing a man among the pigs. He'd been dressed in a pig skin and moved the swine like a general. If there were intelligent forces at work, not just the mindless hunger of animals, everyone needed to stay inside El Cenizo until plans were formed, the mayor told her. None dared admit Pulga was probably dead.

The pigs had been huge, even by the mutant standards of the Frontera, and it had taken four men to move the one pig in town. After it was burned in a pit, the curandera found over twenty bullets among the ashes. If the pigs had found the boy... The Frontera had never been a forgiving place, even before the bombs.

Though the boy's disappearance weighed heaviest on the mother, the mayor felt it too. When he'd been elected, Mayor Flores had wanted to shout, "No! No! No! Anyone but me!" But he'd taken the position because his father told him a true man didn't chase his desires but his purpose. Some said his compassion made him a good leader. Mayor Flores felt it was exactly what would kill him.

Each failed crop, torn fishing net, or thunderstorm caused hair to fall from his head and turned his bowels to water. The deaths made him want to crawl to NEO-Laredo to die alone. Though the Frontera was dangerous and mean, Mayor Flores felt responsible for every snakebite and every illness. He hardly slept and that was before he had to worry about glowing pigs eating his constituents.

The mayor sat in the cool dark of his office when the bell rang on the walls. Thinking it was warning of another disaster, his heart sank. He put on his short-brimmed hat and went out into the blazing afternoon sun.

The excited men on the walls shouted at the gatemen below. Those men wouldn't usually open the gates without instructions, yet they worked in tandem to open them as quickly as the old gears allowed.

A stranger walked through the gates. He was a large dark man, strongly built and broad shouldered. He wore a dusty sarape trimmed by embroidered jaguars and had on thick pants and travel-worn boots. His face was hidden by a luchador's mask—green with flaring eyes and a mouth decorated with jagged designs like teeth. Across his back was strung a two-handed macuahuitl, the obsidian edged sword-club of ancient raza, and on his hip hung a stone dagger.

Yet, it was not his dress, his features, the strange weapons, nor the dried blood on his sarape that captivated the men on the wall. It was the boy in his arms.

"It's Pulga!" they sang. "It's Pulga!"

The stranger gently gave the boy up, telling them Pulga needed water, and went in search of the cantina.

There were cheers once word circulated that the boy was alive and being tended to by the curandera.

Mayor Flores didn't join in the mirth.

He was thankful Pulga was alive, but the boy had needed medicine and supplies, valuable and rare things El Cenizo would need in the coming days. While the town celebrated, Mayor Flores found his way to the cantina, a two-story monstrosity of repurposed wood and steel. The bottom floor served as the bar, cable spool tables spread throughout with a thorny mesquite bartop along the side wall. Upstairs were a few rooms that, with their small cots and tiny windows, were no better than cells.

The mayor was glad the place was nearly empty. Santiago stood behind the bar, resting his eyes, while three old men huddled together, scrutinizing the stranger in the corner eating a plate of nopales. Mayor Flores went over to the bar.

"What'll it be, Mayor?" Santiago said without opening his eyes.

"Double of mezcal," he said, knocking the bar top with his knuckles, instantly snatching his hand away to extract a splinter.

Santiago pushed himself off the wall and limped toward the bottles. He was a stout man with thick wrists and a childhood scavenging the Frontera had claimed his foot, which Santiago replaced with a modded coyote skull. Its jaw clicked whenever he walked.

When he came back with the bottle and poured a glass, the mayor drank it quickly. The mayor held back the water in his eyes and shut his mouth against the rising heat in his guts. "Another," he gasped. "So, tell me..."

Santiago poured. "About what?"

"The stranger. He brought Pulga back, you know?"

"That a fact?" Santiago asked, nodding. "I guess that's what all the cheering was about. I'll have to give him a bottle in thanks."

"I'll give it to him," the mayor said, gesturing impatiently for the bottle. The prospect of having to talk to the stranger—and his macuahuitl—made the mayor want a bottle to himself.

Santiago gave him an unopened bottle of laguna sweet grass wine.

"He wanted a room, I take it," the mayor said. "How'd he pay?"

Santiago sucked his teeth. He fished something out of his pocket and put a solid piece of silver on the bar top.

The mayor scooped it up and examined it. Instead of any minter's mark he'd seen on the Frontera, he found ancient and minute codices, the shapes of eagles and serpents. "What did he tell you?" he whispered.

"He told me he wanted a room and meals," Santiago answered, settling once more onto his place on the wall. "Then he put that in my hand. So, I told the wife to bring him a plate and a key to room three."

The mayor cursed under his breath and drank. He shivered as the mezcal splashed into his stomach. He took the wine over to the stranger who now seemed even larger than before. He didn't look up at the mayor's approach.

"Hello, I'm Mayor Flores, elected leader of El Cenizo," he started. "Santiago, the owner, wanted me to give you this as a thank you for saving Pulga, the boy." He placed the bottle on the table.

The stranger chewed on in silence, hardly glancing at the mayor.

"May I sit?"

"It's your town," the stranger told him. His voice was forceful like waves crashing against a beach.

"We're all very grateful you saved Pulga," the mayor went on. "We'd secretly given up hope."

"I was lucky to spot the boar when I did."

"So you saw one of them?" the mayor said, scoffing. "Horrible beasts, mutated and—How…"

"It was face-first in a hole," the stranger replied. "Its head was buried in the dirt so it was easy to sneak up on it. Blacktooth handled the rest." He reached behind him to his macuahuitl leaning against the wall and tapped the flat of it.

"You killed one? *Alone*?" The mayor was shocked. "The riflemen barely took one down."

The stranger didn't respond.

"Um, please, I don't want you to think we're ungrateful, but… I have to ask, well, *how* you came to find this boar? It was nearby, I'd imagine," Mayor Flores said, tensing with each word.

"I was given a vision and followed it," the stranger said, giving no further explanation.

"You had a vision… of Pulga?"

"No, I didn't *have* a vision, I was *given* one by the old gods of Aztlán," the stranger said between bites. "And the vision wasn't of the boy but of this town. It was being swallowed by a green flood. Finding the boy was luck. Had I come from further west, I'd've missed him."

"And… why would these old gods give you a… vision?" the mayor asked.

"Because I am Cipactli the Blacktooth, one of Aztlán's guerreros," he said. "I was sent into the ruined world to help the lost raza return to The Place That Was Promised, to Aztlán."

The mayor coughed and scooted his chair out. "Well, whoever you are, I thank you again for saving Pulga. Call on me if you need anything and consider yourself our honored guest... from Aztlán."

After he left the cantina, Mayor Flores found a few strong men and went out to find the boar the guerrero had killed. Mayor Flores clutched his stomach the whole walk. The talk of visions and floods, the storybook home of la raza, matched with the guerrero's size and barbaric weapon, threatened to burn a hole in his intestines.

A kettle of vultures led them to Geronimo's Ditch, where a wake of them tore at the remains of a boar. One shot from a rifle scattered the birds, though the vultures perched on the surrounding trees, waiting for the men to finish their business. The boar had nearly been chopped in half, spine and all. From the marks on the ground, not only had the guerrero killed it in one swing, he'd moved all five hundred pounds of it without help.

The mayor clenched his guts and told the men to go back behind the walls. He'd wanted to investigate further, but the realization that the guerrero had that kind of strength made his guts bubble.

IV.

Dolores hurriedly hid her tears when Pulga woke up. She fed him a simple meal of beans fried in grease and ran her fingers through his hair until he was fast asleep again. He'd kept all his food down and already some of his color returned. Afterwards, she went next door and asked la vecina to keep an eye on Pulga while she looked for the guerrero. She hadn't yet thanked him.

She found Cipactli walking along the interior walls. Not far behind were Don Fonseca and some of his followers, whispering that the guerrero might be a bandit looking for weak spots in the wall, but Dolores paid them little attention.

After the town had elected Mayor Flores instead of Don Fonseca, he'd tried—and often—to find any justification to cause a stink. Most of El Cenizo saw it for what it was. A bitter man with little influence puffing his chest. Though she knew he'd try, Dolores had a hard time believing the town would turn on the guerrero who'd saved one of their own, especially a child.

As it was, travelers were rare in the Frontera. The only people that weren't from El Cenizo were traders or merchants from

Viejo Zapata, some as far north as Cotulla. In the world King Gringo ruined, people banded together to survive the harsh land because to brave the ruined world alone was usually a brief and foolish adventure.

But, looking at Cipactli, she thought his large frame and the macuahuitl across his back made him capable of surviving the Frontera alone. The mask she took as the touch of the ruined world, that smudge of madness stamped on all of them. Perhaps it hid a deformity or jagged scars. Whatever the reason, let him keep it, she thought.

"Excuse me, señor," she said, touching his arm. It felt solid like a tree.

He studied Dolores without a hint of lewdness in his dark eyes.

"I'm Dolores La Mantia. Pulga's mother," she said.

"How is the boy?" he asked.

"As well as can be expected," she replied, looking down to hide her welling tears. "They say he almost died from heat. I can't..." She wiped her eyes. "I wanted to thank you. We... we don't have much, but I would like you to eat dinner with us tonight."

The guerrero considered her words and grinned. He wore the expression like a new pair of boots. "That isn't necessary. I'll be happy for a free meal but all I did was my duty," he said.

"Is this... also part of that duty?" she asked, pointing at the walls.

Cipactli nodded. "When I found your boy, the boar was covered in thorns."

He stopped, seeing Dolores's face pale. Still, he continued. "Seeing the outer wall, the pigs that charged your gates were weakening the defenses. The thorns got in their eyes, their snouts, but they'll get closer next time. They may even breach the walls."

"Next time…," she repeated.

"They'll be back," the guerrero said. "I hope the walls will hold. There are some rusted spots in need of repair." He gave her a serious look. "Those pigs, they're not just starving animals. They're smart. They'll come back any day now," Cipactli said, his attention returning to the walls. "But don't worry. I wouldn't be worth my rank if a host of pigs could give me a flowery death."

"I never even asked your name," Dolores stammered, trying to steady herself against the thought of those glowing pigs at the walls again.

"It is long and filled with meaningless titles," he said.

"I'd like to know it all the same."

"My name is Cipactli the Blacktooth, guerrero of Aztlan, chosen of Tlaloc, god of storm and sea," he told her absently.

Dolores blinked through the title. "I thank you again, Cipactli the Blacktooth. Please, tonight, bring your appetite."

"That's one thing I always carry," Cipactli said as he reached out to test the density of a section of wall. He scowled at its flimsiness.

V.

The pig man realized how much he cared for his sounder as he tweezed the last thorns from their hides with his fingers. They were a hard bunch to keep in line. The boars challenged him constantly, more so whenever they had to resort to eating their own. But food was scarce and swine were plentiful. By degrees, the sounder had gotten smaller and smaller until they barely numbered a few hundred. With the coming days, the pig man knew the pigs would need all their strength. El Cenizo was fortified and the people had guns, both powder and lasbolt. Many pigs would die, he knew, patting a passing sow. But once the walls were breached, the pig man could properly bury the fallen instead of butcher them for meat.

The pig man walked among them, his new rebar and concrete hammer in his hands. Some had taken the brunt of the thorns and now, their eyes were useless, their snouts so swollen they could hardly breathe. He knew it was a mercy but that didn't make his task any easier.

He found one, a heavy sow, and touched her. The pig man stopped just short of petting the beast. He reminded himself the world King Gringo ruined was a place of hard decisions. He told it goodbye.

The strike was hard, followed by a wild yell of anguish that was at once human and animal. The pig man struck the sow three more times to be certain she didn't linger.

Wiping the blood off his hands on the rough fur of his rotten boar skin, the pig man saw another—a thorn-covered boar with a nopal paddle lodged in its jaws—and went to it.

Behind him, pigs began to sniff the dead sow.

VI.

Cipactli seemed to fill the entire dining room, dwarfing the small table that was usually enough for Dolores and Pulga. As the boy had healed, the town banded together and brought plates of this and bowls of that to the La Mantias. Dolores knew she and Pulga couldn't possibly finish all the food, so she told Cipactli to eat his fill and to consider it a favor to her.

The guerrero, though, ate no more than them. It hadn't taken him long to see El Cenizo was a town surviving not thriving. Yet, throughout his meal, Cipactli smiled at Pulga, whose energy had returned and brought a childish array of questions. After a while, Dolores told her son he could ask one more question if Cipactli permitted.

The boy frowned as he thought. He'd already asked how Cipactli came to find him, what Aztlán was, and all about the pigs that attacked. "OK," the boy said finally. "What's that thing? If you're a holy guerrero, why'd the gods send you out with a stick?"

"Pulga!" Dolores blurted, shocked.

The guerrero laughed. Motioning to the macuahuitl leaning in the corner, he said, "That's no stick, child. That's Black-tooth. It is a macuahuitl, sword of your people, though that one is larger than most. That was a gift from Tlaloc, god of storm and sea. The wood came from the oldest tree in Aztlán. The stones come from the hearts of our holy mountains. It will never break, the stones form an edge better than steel, and"—he leaned in close, eyes shifting around the room—"it can conjure storms, storms that could flood this whole town. Sometimes, it can even call lightning."

Pulga's eyes got big, but then he looked at the macuahuitl. It looked like carved wood and stone and a leather grip. "You're a liar," he said.

Dolores was horrified. "I'm sorry," she stammered. "My son must've hit his head before you helped him, otherwise he'd never be so *rude*."

Smiling, Cipactli put up his hand. "I've been called worse. But I assure you, I'm not lying."

Pulga crossed his arms. "Show me then."

Cipactli crossed his arms, too, mimicking the boy. "No."

Pulga deflated. "C'mon, if you're not—"

"Boy, I hope you never have to see that as anything but some rocks tied to a stick," Cipactli said. "Because if you see the true gifts of Tlaloc, then I must be in trouble."

The boy's face crinkled.

"OK, Pulga, why don't you clear the table," Dolores said. "Then, go over to Sandra's. Tell her to watch you for a few hours. Don't stray, intiendes? She's expecting you."

"Yes, Ma," Pulga said, collecting the plates for the compost bucket outside. He came back to rinse the plates and put them in the cupboard. Before he left, he thanked Cipactli again.

"Portarse bien," Dolores warned. "Recovering or not, I told Sandra she can whip you."

Pulga rolled his eyes. "Yes, Ma," he said, stomping out with his head thrown back and arms dangling.

Once Pulga was gone, Dolores motioned for Cipactli to stay a moment. She went to the doors, locked them, and went about the small house, turning off lights until the place was sufficiently dim. Slowly, eyes averted, she stood in front of the guerrero. "I want to thank you," she whispered, still unable to look him in the eye.

"You already have."

"No," she persisted. "I want to thank you... properly." She pulled her dress up over her head and placed it, folded, on the table. Her hands inched from her side to cover her nudity but, trembling, she resisted.

Cipactli towered over her.

Dolores winced and it embarrassed her. "I'm sorry, I haven't... not with anyone since my husband..."

Cipactli took the dress off the table and placed it against her. "Clothe yourself."

Dolores looked up, wondering if this guerrero, too, was somewhat ashamed by her offer. But she found that he was looking right at her with unwavering eyes. He'd seen her—all of her—and had not turned away. Still, she was confused. Any man in town would've gone to bed with her and plenty tried after the fever killed her husband.

Cipactli put his hands on her shoulders. "You are a daughter of Aztlán, The Land That Was Promised, where the gods still bless the earth and sky," he said in earnest. "To thank me, raise your son, raise him so the blood of Aztlán lives on. Do that and I'll know my sacrifices—including this one—were not pointless."

Dolores couldn't fight her tears.

Cipactli embraced her. "No, no, no," he soothed. "Don't cry. Not anymore. Aztlán heard your weeping and sent—"

Bells clanged and claxons screeched. There were shouts and a great panic.

"The bells! They've come back!" Dolores shrieked and would've run out to retrieve her son in the nude had Cipactli not held her in place.

"Get dressed and take Pulga to the highest ground you can," the guerrero told her.

She nodded.

Cipactli muttered a prayer to Tezcatlipoca to watch over Dolores and her son and then was gone, macuahuitl in tow.

VII.

The pig man led his swine to the dark just beyond the lights of El Cenizo. He knew the people there could see the green glow of the pigs, of his own flesh. Grunting at his army for them to follow, the pig man walked toward the gates with his hands up. The fear in the faces of those atop the walls was delicious. They were the white eyes and quivering stances of prey.

Once close enough to hear him, he spoke. In the decades among the swine, he'd spoken to them, but the words and structures of language had distorted. "Town surrounded by pig's mine," he said.

He waited.

Seeing he hadn't been shot, he continued. "Boss bring here to listen," he told them.

"We can tell him just fine," one man said. He was puny and old with a long, thin spear.

The pig man squealed in anger. "You tell boss my pigs hungry," he shouted. "Many hungry pigs." He pointed up at the man and stood straighter, revealing himself. The man on the wall was taken aback by the filthy pig man in rags and boarskin, broken skull atop his deformed head like a helmet. Though grown thin, his gaunt frame was made of iron and knotted wood, his teeth chipped down to fangs.

"I am pig now but am people too," the pig man barked, pounding his chest. "We want food. Give it. If no food, give us people. Old. Sick people. You feed or we eat all. Tomorrow, by moon, decide. No give, then take. Take everything."

The pig man put his hands up again, backing away from the walls. He pointed at the guard who'd spoken to him, making a silent promise that when he returned, the pig man would look for that man first. With a few clicks of his tongue, boars and sows stopped sniffing at the ground and followed the pig man back into the dark.

Safely away, a sea of green waves all about him, the pig man made a shrieking, guttural sound and the rest of his sounder took it up like a battle cry. Somewhere on the other side of the town, more pigs took up the horrid song and, as one, the ocean of swine cascaded over the hills and through the trails, wild with the lusty desire to pour over the walls of El Cenizo and flood the town with death.

VIII.

When Cipactli saw the men clustered around one gate, he ran to the southern wall which had needed repairs. At Cipactli's warning, their reply was that the wall faced Viejo Zapata, a friendly city, and would hold against the pigs. But, after hearing the voice beyond the wall, Cipactli realized he wasn't dealing with wild animals that could be baited or thrown into chaos. The pigs were being led by a man who'd managed to survive in the world King Gringo ruined long enough to make pets of the man-eaters.

The guerrero had to treat this new foe as he would any other with ruthless cunning. When the pigs attacked originally, it had been a test to see which sides were most heavily defended and which walls were the strongest. Cipactli was sure the pig man had seen what he'd seen too and the guerrero could only hope to get there in time.

All around El Cenizo, the pigs squealed and belched like an angry, sentient sea.

Cipactli found the southern gate in a panic. Though barred with metal poles, a dozen men held the heavy doors in place.

Among the men were spearmen and riflemen ready to kill anything that might squeeze through. From the gates above, spearmen jabbed their long poles at the clustering swine, scoring superficial wounds that only made them angry. A few had their spears torn from their hands and one unlucky soul was pulled over the wall where he met a swift and violent end—torn to pieces before the dying scream fully escaped his throat.

Cipactli pushed past the men on the ground and bounded up the stairs leading to the parapets. From there, he tried to gauge the enemy but was struck silent and still by the sight, the same he'd seen in his vision. The pigs covered the landscape as their green silhouettes moved in and out of sight like ghosts.

The guerrero's awe was short-lived.

Stacked along the walls were heavy stones to drop on enemies in case of attack. Cipactli lifted a stone the size of a pumpkin over his head, shouting, "To Mictlan with the lot of you!" He threw it with such force, the stone drove a boar's head into the earth, the impact rippling along the wall. The pig's death roused a fire in the spearmen. The monsters in the night were nothing more than livestock, they reminded themselves.

Cipactli rained stones on the pigs trying to force the gate open by sheer numbers. Each stone broke spines and legs, split skulls. But even to the guerrero, it felt that for every pig he killed or rendered useless, two more sprinted in from the dark. He'd almost fallen into a rhythm when gunfire from below cut through his trance.

While the spearmen concentrated on the southern gate, a group of boars wedged one of their heads into a seam in the wall. It snapped and thrashed, letting out an awful stream of squeals that panicked the men. They fumbled with their spears, grazing and nicking the beast, but never braving its proximity enough to kill it.

Cipactli ran along the wall and leaped off it when he was above the fray. Gripping his macuahuitl with both hands, Cipactli chopped and the heavy blow, matched with the momentum of his descent, tore the face off the boar in a single, garish stroke. Cipactli straightened, warning the others. "They know it's there. More will come."

The swine's shoulders and neck were already shaking in the seam. The pigs behind the dead boar ate it until it was nothing.

"Spears! One to each side and one dead on," Cipactli said, pantomiming a spear thrust. "Rifles, go in between them. Don't waste bullets. You'll need every one of them. Shoot only when you have a shot."

The men traded determined nods. Hearing a simple plan and seeing a boar killed so easily softened the invasion to something like a routine, like pruning nopales or walking the walls.

Cipactli left them to regroup. He thought of going back to the wall to kill more pigs from above, but shouts from the east had him running hard, wondering what new threat the green sea posed. When he neared the eastern gate, he wasn't sure how, but pigs scaled the wall, single file, spilling over the lip. The closer he got, Cipactli heard shouts the pigs used their dead to climb over a low spot on the wall.

One had already tumbled into El Cenizo. The pig chased and charged at a panicked group of men who half-heartedly corralled it with their speartips. The rifles were engaged with boars and pigs making their ascension on the backs of the dead. A huge boar flopped onto the ramparts and scattered the riflemen before righting itself.

Shouting a war cry of Aztlán, the guerrero ran to the scene, hoping to get the pig's attention.

Sensing a greater threat, the pig swung around and barreled through the loose ring of men. It met the guerrero with jaws open and snapped at Cipactli's guts.

Cipactli put both hands on either end of his macuahuitl and wedged it into the pig's open mouth like a horse's bit. The beast's momentum drove the obsidian edges deep into its face. Sure that the ancient weapon was firmly in the beast's mouth, Cipactli took the handle in both hands and pulled it free, stone edges shredding pork down to the beast's neck. But the guerrero had no time to catch his breath.

The boar on the ramparts found its way to the ground and swung a spearman by a mangled leg. Cipactli had no way to reach the man in time, so he took his macuahuitl in both hands and pitched it end over end, following as fast as his aching legs allowed.

The macuahuitl's edge bit into the boar's neck just beneath the jaw. Letting the injured man fly, it squealed with rage. The boar spotted Cipactli and, like its fellow, charged. The boar, with its sheer size and fury, wasn't concerned with tactics.

As it approached, Cipactli cursed his luck that the stuck macuahuitl hadn't killed the boar outright and brandished the only weapon he had left. A stone dagger. He held it out in front of him, waiting for the boar's next move.

The sight of Cipactli standing in defiance slowed the boar's charge by a step. The hesitation gave the guerrero a chance to slash the stone dagger across the boar's snout, slicing a bloody line across its nostrils. The boar made a chilling sound and bit, but Cipactli was beside it, flicking the stone blade quickly. The boar felt painful lines flare across its neck and face and the sting and blindness that came from its eye bursting after one deft swipe.

The boar spun around in a frenzy, trying to catch Cipactli, but the guerrero was always ahead of it, scoring cut after cut, until the boar looked to be of two faces, one of ribboned flesh and the other of a deformed boar. But, with each spin, the weaker the boar became until, finally, it bit and chased only out of sheer stubbornness. By then, some of the spearmen arrived and helped bleed the animal to death.

Cipactli thanked them and ripped his macuahuitl from the boar's neck. He wiped his dagger on the boar and replaced it in his belt. He swung his macuahuitl in a low arc, smashing open the top of the boar's skull, showering one man with blood and brains. Cipactli looked at him and, in apology, said, "You can't be too careful."

The guerrero left the dead boar and readied himself for another animal to drop from the ramparts. A huge pig emerged from the other side of the wall and seized a spear in its jaws when the pig man's call cut through even the cacophony of war.

The beast dropped out of sight and the men on the wall shouted reports that the pigs were retreating toward NEO-Laredo.

El Cenizo cheered, yet Cipactli didn't join them.

He'd heard the pig man's words. The green sea would return. They'd seen the defenses, tested the gaps. Cipactli switched his grip on his macuahuitl and collected a lantern. When the enemy retreated, it was wise to plan and repair, so spoke the old gods of Aztlán.

IX.

After spending the rest of the night marking the walls for repairs and making note of the piles of dead pigs to be burned, Cipactli had a heavy slumber full of dreams. He dreamed of Aztlán, of its lost raza all over the ruined world, and how a tide of green threatened to swallow them up. All of it, Cenizo, Aztlán, the world. He woke lathered in sweat. Once he got his bearings, Cipactli laughed to himself, thinking it foolish that a few hundred pigs could create so much dread within him.

Outside his room, Cipactli couldn't make them out, but people were giving passionate speeches about something.

The guerrero put on his boots and left his room, leaning on the banister overlooking the interior of the cantina. Most of the men and some of the women were there, filling the room with smoke and fiery words. The mayor, too, was there, looking ill, while another man stood addressing the people.

"—would be to let us all die," the other man said, giving the mayor a contemptuous look. The man was fatter than even the laziest in Aztlán, which there were few, and he wore a neatly pressed set of clothes to match his gleaming metal smile. "I may not have what the rest of you do—family, children, parents still living—but I consider all of you my family. I'd do anything for you, for the wellbeing of everyone in El Cenizo. We should demand everyone do the same."

"Do you understand what you're saying?" Mayor Flores shouted, the effort making him woozy. "What you're asking people to do? Yes, paint it however you want, but you're saying, why not give them the old. What are they worth? And the sick. Neither can work, neither contributes, so just... just... send them out to be eaten alive? If you're so eager, who gets to say what's a contribution or what's useful, huh, Fonseca? Say... What exactly do *you* do?" the mayor went on, pointing at the fat man, who looked appalled by the question.

"Why, my organizational and managerial skills are—"

"Bullshit!" the mayor cried, steadying himself. "You goddamn coward—"

"Mayor or not, I won't be talked to—"

"It's true! Where were you last night? Which wall?" the mayor asked. "You'd feed us all to those pigs by hand if you could get out of it alive. We won't allow one person to die by those pigs, not willingly."

"You won't *allow* it?" Fonseca shot back. "How many are dead? Answer me. Ten. Two on the first night. Eight last night, not including Richie with his leg torn off or Celso with his hip cracked. And how many did *we* get," he asked, emphasizing his own inclusion though Cipactli couldn't recall seeing Fonseca the night before. "How long can we truly last against them?

One attack? Two, maybe. Then we'll all be dead. But if we give them—"

"We'll give them nothing but steel and fire," Cipactli said, drawing everyone's attention.

"Go back to sleep, *friend*," Don Fonseca spat. "This matter doesn't concern an outsider."

"Hey, if it wasn't for him, Richie'd be dead," one of the spearmen put in. Others agreed.

Cipactli went down to them and stood near Don Fonseca, dwarfing the man. "A creature, more pig than man, said these things," Cipactli reasoned. "He told you he wants supplies and a few people in exchange for your safety. That's all. And let's say you do give up a few, perhaps he'll be true to his word and leave. What then? You bargained with *one* man. How many *pigs* were there? Hundreds. Under his control or not, they are animals. And they are starving. He told us so himself. What pig rations supplies? What pig eats only enough to survive and then moves so another can eat? To give in will give you another few days before he demands more and more, until there is no one left to fight and then he'll take all of you. Like a flood. They will not stop until they are stopped."

Fonseca scoffed. "And how do you intend we do that? Not all of us can kill a pig in one stroke like you."

"I have a plan," Cipactli said. "We know what they'll exploit, so we can be ready for that. As for the rest, we need Black-tooth." He lifted the macuahuitl for all to see, to marvel at the images of Tlaloc and his wife Chalchiuhtlicue adorning the flat of it.

"A *stick* will save us then?"

"And river fish," Cipactli replied, lowering his weapon. "The fresher the better."

X.

An armed detail went with a few men to get fish from the rio. They returned with a dozen in buckets from which Cipactli selected nine, asking that they be preserved in a tank. The rest of the day was spent doing an inventory of the entire town, gathering wood and metal for either reinforcement or active defense. Lamp oil and bottles were lined up on the walls. Throughout the preparations, Cipactli never stopped to rest and only ate because an old woman persistently offered him homemade guisado. "Sin puerco," she assured him.

He ate enough to be polite then found an excuse to help the men outside clear the pig carcasses. The piles were large, but the number, to the town's dismay, was less than they'd hoped. Still, it was disgusting work that went faster with Cipactli's bull-strength. He moved the bodies far from the gates and proceeded to butcher them, scattering the rotting pieces. "They're hungry," he told a curious group who gave him strange looks. "Put food out for them. They'll be distracted."

The men didn't say anything, placing a dead sow a few paces away and hacking it to pieces.

Cipactli returned to El Cenizo but refused even to sit in the shade awhile. The holes in the walls were plugged and reinforced and the tops were lined with firebombs and heavy stones. The women and children had been taken to the church's belfry, the stairs of which had been removed after them.

After all the preparations had been done, Cipactli asked that the fish be taken to the center of town, where he spread out a piece of carpet. Burying the top of his macuahuitl in the ground beside it, he sat there cross-legged, eyes closed to the intense daylight. The words Cipactli spoke comforted and energized those who heard him though they didn't understand. Cipactli made sweeping, pious gestures, begging the old gods.

From behind his window overlooking the town center, Don Fonseca scoffed, saying, *"That's* who they listen to? Christ, he should be the first one we give up." Clicking his teeth, he watched Cipactli pluck a fish from the tank and offer it up to the sky. With his finger, the guerrero pierced the fish's belly, dug through the innards, and pulled out what Don Fonseca could only guess was the heart.

The guerrero set the fish heart on the carpet in front of him and brought the dead fish to his forehead before tossing it aside. He did the same for the other eight, the prayer and piercing, the removal of their hearts. By the ninth fish, the sky was a pastel colorscape and the men on the walls kept a nervous eye out for the pigs.

No one dared ask what Cipactli was doing.

The guerrero took the nine hearts and ate them, letting the watery blood stain the teeth of his mask. Gracefully, he got to his feet and pulled the macuahuitl out of the ground. He whipped the weapon around with deft, precise motions, each movement causing his prayers to get louder. The chant filled the square, filled the town. The rhythm grew heavy and intense, ending with a word that the town grew to understand. Tlaloc, god of storm and sea.

To those enthralled by the ritual, it was like Cipactli changed day into night. They looked up to the dark sky and found the few lonely wisps of clouds above were inflating into steely purple behemoths, bellies alive with lightning. All around El Cenizo, the shadows of the clouds drew their attention, hypnotizing them with their lights and the rumble of thunder so close the air rattled within their chests.

Through it all, Cipactli stretched his arms up to the storm clouds as if trying to embrace them. He held that pose until the rain came. At first, it was the gentle drizzle that often teased the Frontera, but soon transformed into fat drops that slapped all the upturned faces.

The people forgot everything for a moment and joined in Cipactli's pose, arms outstretched and palms upturned. They smiled as the cool water wet their lips and rubbed the dirt from their faces. A few even laughed.

A warning bell rang on the northern wall and Cipactli went to heed its call, to face the beasts outside among the mud and meat.

XI.

The first ranks of pigs went at the rotten meat, bullying and fighting one another for the choicest cuts. From the way they bled into the open land outside El Cenizo's walls, Cipactli had been correct to anticipate their gluttony. The rain, too, disrupted their march. The clay soil turned slick. Still, to the men on the walls, the sounder did look like the sea come to meet them, an endless sway of green light beneath a stormy sky. The dark made their numbers hard to see except by lightning. With each burst of light, there were more and more trotting to devour them.

Wild from the stink of the rotten meat and the promise of food, the quickest pigs broke away from the others, darting for the nearest target, Cipactli, who'd gone outside to meet them and possibly gain his flowery death.

Cipactli cut through them, severing the legs of one boar with a backhanded cut and shearing off the top of a sow's skull with a slash. By lightning, the pigs charged him, hooves unsteady on the slippery ground, but the guerrero was ahead of them at every step. Each swing of his macuahuitl killed and maimed, taking the eyes of one, the jaw of another. He fought ferociously, the pile of dead swine growing, drawing in more, their unity disrupted by the chance to feast.

Some of the pigs rushed the walls, ramming the seams in the welding again and again, and paid the guerrero no attention at all. Those pigs were stung by spears—all bullets were to be saved until needed same with lasrifle powercells—and showered by firebombs which burned despite the rain. The men knew none of it mattered to the pigs. This was not a war of men but the survival of beasts. Both sides were fighting for their very lives.

The pigs testing the defenses came in succession, a troop of sows spread thin to test the walls to see which spots had more give than the rest, and they were followed by a team of boars that threw their bodies at the walls. Each impact rumbled up through the boots of all who stood on the ramparts.

Dire as it was, those in view of the field kept chancing glances at the spectacle there.

Amidst the rolling green was a giant, spreading death with each pass of his macuahuitl, the blood of half a dozen wounds washed clean by rain of his own creation. For as heroic a sight as it was, those who saw it wondered how long it could last. Giant, guerrero, paladin of Aztlán, Cipactli was still a man.

The pigs died by the second but were replaced even before they stopped thrashing on the ground. It would only be a matter of time before one bite was too much or one swing too slow, then the people would return to surviving alone, abandoned by Aztlán and the old gods again.

Cutting through the thunder, through the bursts of bombs and endless squeals, those on the wall heard Cipactli call out in his ancient tongue. "Tlapepetlani," he roared.

Lightning answered his call.

The bolt enveloped the guerrero and scattered the pigs. A few were scorched to death, blackened skin crackling against the rain, while others were knocked deaf and blind, left to shamble through their swarming fellows. More still felt the residual shock of the white-hot bolt. They convulsed and seized in the mud, kicking their legs frantically and thrashing on their backs.

Those stunned were the first to be slain, then those that wandered in the direction of the piles of dead. Scorched as the point of impact had been and wide as the affected circle was, the steaming guerrero emerged from it with frightening ease, leaving his ring of death to wade into the thicket of swine, flanking them. Bellies were torn open, legs freed from bodies, until Cipactli called the lightning once more.

It came so close to the walls, men ducked to avoid it, thinking the old gods meant to kill them too. But when the thunder no longer shook, they peered over the walls and saw that the bolt had ripped one pig to pieces and scorched a dozen more.

The pigs were in chaos, dying one by one as Cipactli cut lines through them. Some of the men on the wall even dared to smile. The old gods of raza were beside them in that dark hour.

Then a wretched and humanoid squeal came from the south, wiping away all smiles.

XII.

No one saw the pig man find his way into El Cenizo. The display of lightning had drawn their attention elsewhere. The men at the southern gate had looked away one moment and, in the next, the pig man was there on the ramparts, swinging his concrete hammer. He knocked riflemen off the wall and deftly dodged the thrusts of spearmen. He got to the ground and ran for the gate controls, swatting men aside.

He killed the man guarding the controls, nearly folding him over with a blow to the top of his skull. The pig man stepped over the body and hammered at the controls, setting the crossbars to shaking and the doors to rattling. As he found the right sequence, the pig man felt something bite into his shoulder. Turning, his hammer slapping the spear aside, the pig man faced the man who dared draw his blood.

To the pig man, Mayor Flores was small, even by human standards, and held a long spear in front of him. Though the mayor's stature and the nervous way the weapon shook in his hand didn't show it, the pig man recognized the way the others voiced their concerns and scrambled to reach Mayor Flores.

Somehow, the twitchy little man who reeked of shit was important, the pig man reasoned and bared his teeth in disgust. Men coddled weakness while his pigs understood only strength.

The mayor thrust the spear at the pig man's face, but the pig man stopped it easily, catching the spear with one hand.

The pig man yanked the spear and struck the shaft, snapping it in two. Smiling, he expected the mayor, now defenseless, to run, but the little man stood there, unmoved. At first, the pig man figured the mayor was paralyzed with fear. Then the mayor lifted his half of the spear and swung it with all his strength and cracked it against the pig man's hip.

Though sudden, the whole thing confused and insulted the pig man. To his sounder, he was an uncrossable creature to be obeyed. Challenged often though he was, the pig man earned his place among the pigs, none of which dared look in his eyes lest he think it rebellion.

Yet, this little man had not only drawn his blood but dared attack him again.

The pig man tossed the spear into the chest of the nearest rifleman and then took his rebar hammer in both hands. The swing came from below, catching the mayor in the ribs and lifting him off his feet. Mayor Flores crashed on the wet ground where he lay still. In that moment, the pig man forgot himself, the plan, and the pigs. The little man had insulted him and the pig man decided the best revenge would be to eat his face.

A lasbolt sizzled the ground at his feet, drawing his attention to a man on the wall. The pig man growled and bounded for the steps, tossing one man aside and knocking another's knee out of place. On the ramparts, the pig man slid over the wall and landed atop a particularly fat boar. Squealing for some to follow, the pig man hunched over, his boar skin blending in with the sea of swine, and led some of the pigs to another wall.

Nearing the next gate, the pig man expected to see his pigs ten-deep pressed against the walls, the men above scrambling in fright. He never thought he'd see a field of slaughtered pigs.

Some still tried their luck with the walls, denting and wedging holes big enough for a pig or two to slip inside. But the majority were at war with a guerrero nearly as tall as he. The guerrero's clothes were torn, cuts and gouges dotting his flesh, and the sword-club in his hands was soaked in blood and fringed with green fur. Piles of dead lay all around him.

Slayer of his pigs or not, the guerrero was engaged with a feisty boar and a sow near-dead, and the pig man moved to attack. But, before he could get close enough, a volley of bullets and lasbolts zipped through the air, felling a nearby pig. A firebomb showered flames close by. The pig man looked again, watched his sounder die, and let out a wild, mournful peal.

Like trained dogs, the pigs went to him, following as the pig man sprinted past the scattered remains for NEO-Laredo.

The pig man hated to retreat but understood it was best. They'd regroup, he'd devise another plan, perhaps surround the town at such a distance that they'd be able to starve them out. Still with tactics in his mind, the pig man stopped a distance from El Cenizo to count the pigs left. He was bothered that they were slow to follow but knew hunger and bloodlust clouded their simple minds.

He counted nearly fifty when the sound of squealing in the distance was cut short by a vicious chop and the loud crack of bone. The pig man growled, knowing the guerrero was trailing his sounder. So be it, he thought, merging with the retreating pigs. If the guerrero wanted to follow them to NEO-Laredo, there he'd only find his doom. His flesh wouldn't feed many pigs, but the pig man swore he'd divide the body so that all could taste the dead guerrero.

XIII.

Cipactli was exhausted. The ritual and the summoning paled in comparison to the toll of non-stop battle, the constant tug of death, the thrusting of the mind into the dangerous realm of reflex and instinct. He wasn't sure how many pigs he'd killed but knew had it not been for the blessings and enchantments of the old gods of Aztlán, he'd've met his flowery death, bite by bite.

Cipactli followed the hundreds of hoofprints and the trail of pig's blood all the way to the edge of NEO-Laredo. He passed pigs fallen over in death, their bodies bloody and pockmarked. Others wandered in the delirium of their final moments.

Cipactli didn't bother them. They posed no threat to anyone and he needed all his strength for the final hunt.

He felt the heat of NEO-Laredo the instant he stepped in it. A warmth that came from the buildings, the ground. Walking through the ruins of blown out structures and fragmented roads, Cipactli thought of all the raza who died there, who had been poisoned by King Gringo's bombs and felt their judging eyes on him. In Aztlán, they'd heard the screams of millions of raza, like the wailing of a nation of ghosts before they were reduced to atoms. It was then that Aztlán revealed itself to the world once more and sent its guerreros to save its lost people. But that was so long ago.

The man he hunted, the guerrero knew, could've been raza once. Now, he was something between man and beast. At some point, Cipactli was sure, the pig man had people and a life, but the bombs stole all of that, leaving a broken city and a broken man. It would be enough to drive any man into the company of glowing swine.

The pigs left fresh tracks through the city up to a gated collection of rotten mansions left to the elements. Cipactli found the huge iron gate knocked over, bent from platoons of pigs trampling it daily. A few of the pigs stood on porches or rested themselves on lawns. None dared approach. They knew why Cipactli was there and watched as he passed, their snouts picking up the scent of death and pig blood.

The guerrero walked through the broken streets, macuahuitl tight in his hands, and scanned the homes for any sign of the pig man. He caught a scent on the wind, a sharp odor like spoiled meat and cloyed fruit. Cipactli followed it, thinking it better than any tracks—the entire area housed the pigs for untold years and tracks and dung covered nearly every inch of the neighborhood. Before long, Cipactli came to the remains of a golf course long overtaken by weeds.

Cipactli walked the gentle hills and kept his eyes on the large homes that he felt bore witness to his weariness. The porches and terraces were all broken and empty, but he still imagined the raza that must've dined there, drank to their luck and fortunes. There was evidence of fires on a veranda. Painted on the roof of another was the word AYÚDANOS!

Cipactli tightened his grip on his macuahuitl, resolving that though Aztlán had been too late for them, he would protect the remaining raza even if it meant his death.

The crescendo of stink told him which mansion held the pig man.

It was the largest of them all, three stories with columns and a pool left to collect stagnant water and pig shit. The fence that blocked it off from the golf course had been knocked over so long ago it nearly melded with the soil. Whatever trees had been there were dead, one knocked over and leaning against the terrace. The windows were gone and the only door remaining hung by one stubborn hinge. The edges of the doorway were scoured free of color from pigs brushing past.

The place was in shambles. A cloud of flies hung over everything, buzzing in and out of holes in the walls and the shredded rugs and furniture streaked with blood and shit. The room he entered was large and opened to the rest of the first floor. A fat staircase led to the second-floor landing.

Cipactli, nearly swooning from the radiating heat, stood there a moment to try to filter out the thousands of tiny wings for any sound that might lead him to the pig man. Slowly, the buzzing became nothing and the sounds of the house were able to slip through.

Unknowing of what could strike at him from the shadows, Cipactli advanced cautiously. He neared the stairs, thinking, perhaps, the pig man wanted the advantage of higher ground. As he decided to take a step, a whisper of coarse hair against a wall caught his ear.

Blacktooth went up by reflex.

For a man starved, poisoned, and gone feral, the pig man was shockingly quick and viciously strong. His concrete hammer clacked against the flat of Cipactli's macuahuitl, knocking it aside. The pig man tried to follow the strike with a backhanded swing for the guerrero's head, but Cipactli rushed in, shouldering the off-balanced pig man back a step. The pig man grunted but had to scramble to dodge the macuahuitl's upward slash.

Still, despite the brute edge of the macuahuitl and the strength of his foe, the pig man did not run. He kicked a pile of filth at the guerrero and was behind it in an instant, hammering at Cipactli from every angle. He felt a few swings connect, but, before long, the guerrero was matching him swing for swing, ducking and countering, catching the edges of the pig man's cloak or mantle before having to avoid the concrete hammer.

Strike by strike, the macuahuitl whittled away at the hammerhead, each scrape and clatter of stone chips only infuriating the pig man further.

Cipactli inwardly smiled, thinking that the pig man's ferocity would somehow leave him open for attack. The weaponmasters of Aztlán taught such tactics. Yet, the guerrero realized in the renewed fury, those were tactics for men not beasts. And the pig man was both... and neither.

The anger only made the pig man faster, more unpredictable. Soon, no longer did Cipactli dictate the motions, guiding the pig man to open himself to a fatal strike, but was reacting, getting his macuahuitl up quick enough to deflect one strike before having to ready himself for another. Each blow sent shockwaves through his hands up to his shoulders, making his arms heavy.

The guerrero's chance came when one of the pig man's swings was short, leaving the deformed man open. Cipactli sent his macuahuitl into a waist-high arc, hoping to gut his enemy. But the wild man was too nimble, hopping out of range and taking his hammer in both hands, lifting it high over his head.

Again, Cipactli rushed in, his own weapon ready to block. Their arms tangled, putting their faces only inches apart. The pig man tried to force his arms down, but Cipactli's strength held. Without warning, the pig man's face shot forward, broken teeth leading.

The guerrero managed to get his forearm in the way and the pig man's jagged teeth sank into the meat of his arm. As the pig man bit down, the guerrero's right hand slipped beneath his sarape and brought out his stone dagger. Cipactli stuck it in the pig man's ribs up to the hilt.

But the deformed man bit down harder and, with a burst of strength, thrashed, sending Cipactli to the ground.

The guerrero hit the floor hard, his body momentarily pulling him to unconsciousness, but he knew any lapse of focus would be his death. Getting a foot under himself, Cipactli swung around, his macuahuitl arcing without aim. He expected it to cut air, to be the last desperate act before the concrete hammer came down on his head and sent him to Mictlan for his failure. But he felt the weapon smash though one of the pig man's arms and bury itself in the man's skull.

Impossibly, the pig man did not fall.

He stood stone still, face bleeding freely, one arm still holding the hammer while the other, now detached, still stubbornly grasped the rebar handle. The pig man's mouth, stopped in time, trembled as if to speak, and all the life rushed from him. He fell at once like his legs and spine liquified.

Cipactli collapsed with him, laying on the filthy floor until his breath steadied. He stood and, planting his foot on the pig man's face to do it, collected his macuahuitl. Looking at the dead man, Cipactli suddenly felt the exhaustion of the days of battle and of the irradiated city. Still, he hacked the head off the pig man's body to be certain he was dead. Then, Cipactli removed the boar skin. He wanted it as proof for El Cenizo and as a talisman against the pigs outside.

He found the skin almost fused to the pig man by pus and grime. What did not come off, he tore free, leaving the headless corpse in flesh-rags on the ground.

The pigs did react to the skin, smelling it and trying to trot after Cipactli, but the guerrero shooed them away with his macuahuitl, which the pigs eyed cautiously before returning to their mansions.

XIV.

They found the guerrero almost a mile from town. Nearly dead, his body was covered in cuts, bruises, and burns from the radiation. Clutched in his hand was a filthy pig's pelt that stank of infection. Some men carried the guerrero inside El Cenizo while a pair set the stinking pelt on fire.

The men laid him on a cot next to the mayor, who had been placed in an iron-lung, his chest nearly caved in while defending the gate.

The curandera removed the guerrero's sarape and found a map of scars beneath it. Marks of blade and fang, fire and set bones, were woven into his flesh. The fresh wounds were cleaned, the broken ribs set, and nearly two hundred stitches were needed, nearly forty were for the garish bite on his arm.

Throughout, weak and delirious as he was, the guerrero never let them remove his mask.

He was slow to recover, his stitches healing well enough, but a sort of sickness hovered over him for days. It was Dolores that called it radiation poisoning, the lingering stink of King Gringo. Cipactli was of Aztlán, she explained, and Aztlán had remained untouched by the bombs. El Cenizo, the world, they'd adapted to the poison or died.

The medicines did little.

It was on the fifth day that the guerrero spoke as if in a dream. "The rio," he said. "Take me…" When they told him to rest, he repeated, "To the rio."

They protested, but the mayor ordered it from his iron-lung. "He saved us… Do as he… Do it," the mayor pressed.

Most of El Cenizo gathered to watch the guerrero's journey to the rio. It wasn't until they dressed him and armed him that they truly noticed the toll the siege and the hunt in NEO-Laredo had taken. Pale and thin, it was Santiago and Dolores who led Cipactli to the water's edge.

Fighting to keep his balance, Cipactli struggled into the rio until it was up to his ribs. When he went under, some called to pull him out, but the guerrero rose, his heavy hands cupping water to clean his mask. His skin had grown darker, the pale harshness of his wounds standing out. Dunking himself into the rio stripped off the layers of illness on him until he stood as he had when he'd brought Pulga back.

He gave El Cenizo a somber, paternal look. "Aztlán waits," he said. "Aztlán will ignore you no longer. Go south and she will find you."

Closing his eyes, Cipactli went further into the rio until it was above his head.

He never came up again.

—ETC.—

About the Cover Artist

William Keops Ibañez was born in the border town of Laredo Texas in 1982. His youth was spent drawing for hours, working at his family's Mexican Restaurant, and attending local Punk shows on San Bernardo Avenue. He graduated from the School of Visual Arts in New York City in 2005 with a B.F.A. in Illustration and Cartooning. His artwork and design has graced apparel from companies such as Gap and Hot Topic among many others. He is currently working on his comic book series *Blazing Quantum, True Tales from La Frontera*. William currently resides in Nueva Jersey with his two kids. Read more at keopsibanez.com.

About the Author

Mario E. Martinez is the author of *San Casimiro, Texas: Short Stories*, *A Pig Named Orrenius & Other Strange Tales*, and *Ashtree*. He lives in South Texas. His works are available at www.marioemartinez.com.